Totline "Take-Home" Books
Color, Shape & Season Rhymes

Circles

Reproducible Pre-Reading Books
For Young Children

(Previously published as part of "Make & Take" Concept Rhymes.)

Written by Jean Warren • Illustrated by Cora Walker-Carleson

Editor: Gayle Bittinger
Layout and Cover Design: Kathy Jones

ISBN 0-911019-28-6

Printed in the United States of America
Published by: Warren Publishing House, Inc.
          P.O. Box 2250
          Everett, WA 98203

Contents

Color Books

Red
Yellow
Blue
Green
Orange
Purple
Brown
Black
White

Shape Books

Circles
Squares
Triangles
Rectangles
Ovals

Season Books

Fall
Winter
Spring
Summer

Introduction

Young children who are just becoming interested in books and reading are usually long on enthusiasm and short on ability. Totline "Take-Home" Books are designed to capture that enthusiasm.

Each pre-reading book centers around a particular learning concept and is written in rhyme. The unique feature of these rhymes is that young children are able to "read" them, using pictures as their guides. This happens because each rhyme is simply written and illustrated with pre-readers in mind. After reading a book with an adult a few times, your children will be able to "read" it by themselves.

Because all of the pre-reading books in this series are reproducible, your children can each have his or her own. And they will glow with pride and feelings of accomplishment as they take home their own books to "read" to their families.

General Directions

- Tear out the pages for the take-home book of your choice.
- Make one photocopy of the book for each child. Cut the pages in half.
- Place the pages on a table and let the children help collate them into books.
- Give each child two 5½- by 8-inch pieces of construction paper to use for book covers.
- Let the children decorate their book covers as desired or use one of the suggestions on the following pages.
- Help the children bind their books using a stapler or a hole punch and brass paper fasteners.

Suggestions for Using the
Color, Shape & Season Rhymes Take-Home Books

The take-home books in *Color, Shape & Season Rhymes* are fun and easy to use. You can enlarge the pages to make big books for your room, introduce the rhymes with flannelboard cutouts, or give out the books at the end of a unit about a particular color, shape or season. Following are suggestions for using the take-home books with preschoolers, kindergarteners and first and second graders. Mix and match the ideas to meet the needs and interests of your children.

Preschool

General Ideas
- Let the children use rubber stamps that correspond with the rhyme's subject to stamp the covers of their books.
- Give the children appropriate stickers to attach to the covers of their books.

Color Books
- Have the children fingerpaint the covers of their books in the appropriate color.
- Cut small pieces from various kinds of paper in the appropriate color. Let the children glue the pieces on their book covers.
- Give the children construction paper book covers, the appropriate color of crayons and a piece of textured material such as sandpaper or needlepoint canvas. Have them make rubbings on their covers.
- Add extra pages to the end of each book. Cut out magazine pictures of objects that are the appropriate color. Have the children glue them to their extra pages. Ask them to name the objects when they read their books.

Shape Books
- Cut out the appropriate shape in various sizes and colors of construction paper. Have the children glue the shapes on the covers of their books.
- Cut sponges into the appropriate shape. Let the children use the sponges like stamps and make designs on their book covers.
- Photocopy each half page on a separate page. Cut the pages into the appropriate shape.
- As you read the rhyme, have the children point to things nearby that are that shape.

Season Books
- Cut fall leaf, winter mitten, spring flower or summer butterfly shapes out of construction paper. Let the children glue the appropriate shapes on their book covers.
- Make paint pads by folding paper towels, placing them in shallow containers and pouring small amounts of tempera paint on them. Give the children cookie cutters that are in shapes that represent the appropriate season. Have the children dip their cookie cutters into the paint and then press them on the covers of their books.

Kindergarten

General

- Have the children write their names on the backs of their books.
- Have the children write the name of the color, shape or season on their book covers.

Color Books

- Have the children color the pictured objects the appropriate color.

Shape Books

- Make a dot-to-dot shape on each child's cover. Have the children follow the dots to create their shapes.
- Draw the appropriate shape on each child's cover. Have the children incorporate the shape into pictures they draw on their covers.
- For each child draw the appropriate shape several times on a piece of construction paper. Give the children the paper and scissors. Let them cut out their shapes and glue them on their book covers.
- Have the children color just the shape each time it appears on the pages in the book.

Season Books

- Have the children glue magazine pictures of the appropriate season on their book covers.

First and Second Grades

General

- Let the children take their books home to color.
- Have the children write "This book belongs to (child's name)" on their back covers.
- Have the children copy each sentence of a particular rhyme onto a separate page. Let them illustrate each of their pages.
- Photocopy each half page on a full sheet of paper with lines for writing practice below the picture. Have the children copy the words on the page.

Color Books

- Add extra pages to the back of each child's book. Let the children cut out magazine pictures of objects that are the appropriate color. Have them write the names of the objects below them.
- Have the children draw the pictures of things that are the appropriate color on the covers of their books.

Shape Books

- Let the children draw pictures on their book covers using only the appropriate shape in various sizes.
- Have the children use pencils or crayons to trace over the dark outlines of the shapes on each page of their books.

Season Books

- Let the children create book covers by drawing pictures of things they like to do in the appropriate season.

Color
Books

Red valentine

Red stop sign

Red strawberry

Red fire engine

Red apple

Red, red, all around.

See the red things I have found.

Yellow sun

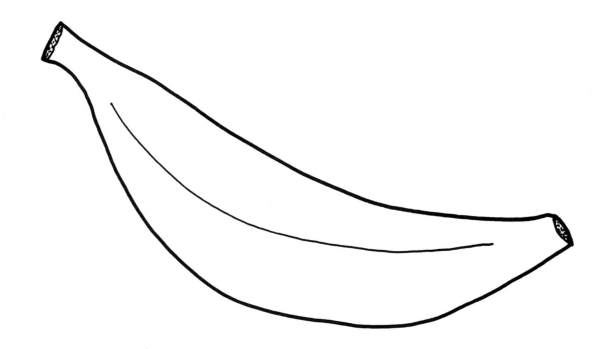

Yellow banana

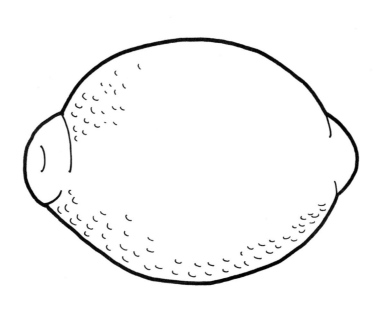

Yellow lemon

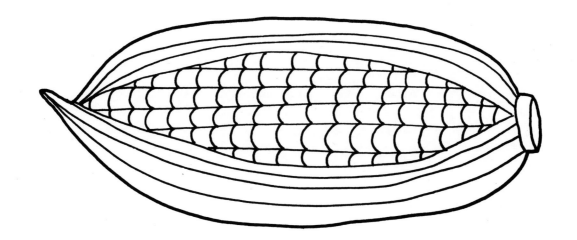

Yellow corn

Yellow chick

Yellow, yellow, all around.

See the yellow things I have found.

Blue blueberries

Blue mailbox

Blue blue jay

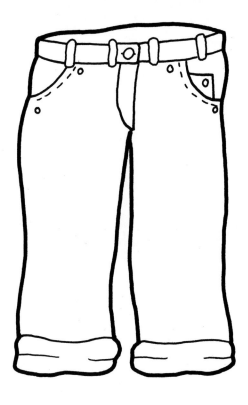

Blue jeans

Blue sea

Blue, blue, all around.

See the blue things I have found.

Green

Green turtle

Green shamrock

Green frog

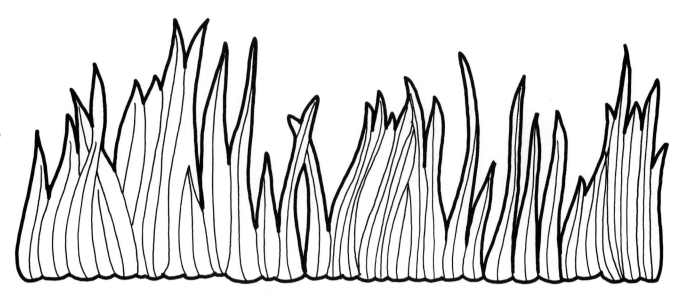

Green grass

Green tree

Green, green, all around.

See the green things I have found.

Orange

Orange pumpkin

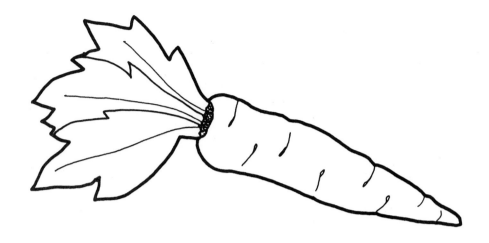

Orange carrot

Orange crab

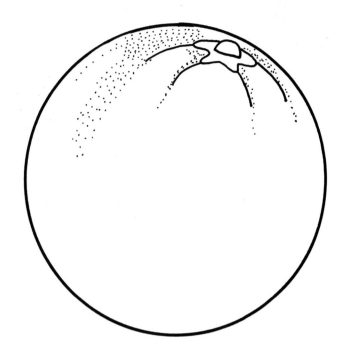

Orange orange

Orange fish

Orange, orange, all around.

See the orange things I have found.

Purple

Purple violets

Purple grapes

Purple plum

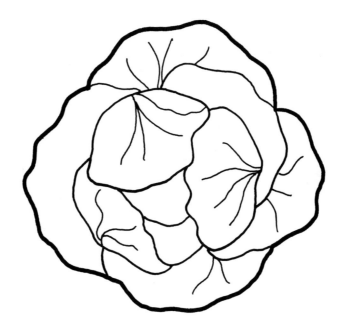

Purple cabbage

Purple juice

Purple, purple, all around.

See the purple things I have found

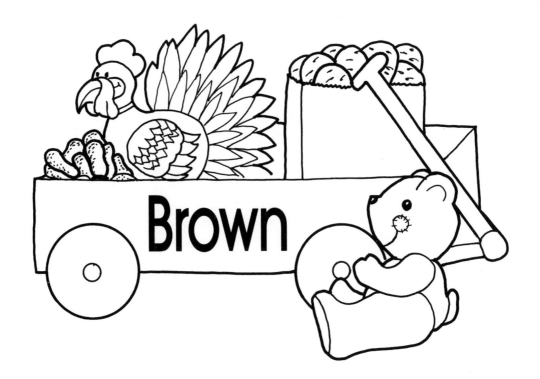

Brown teddy bear

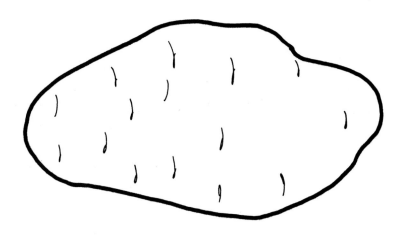

Brown potato

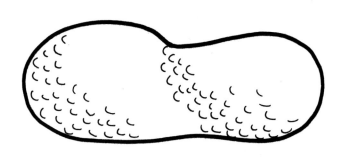

Brown peanut

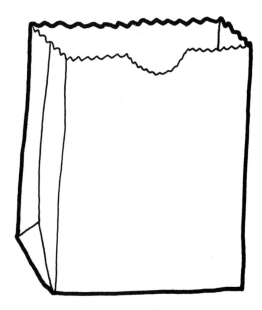

Brown bag

Brown turkey

Brown, brown, all around.

See the brown things I have found.

Black spider

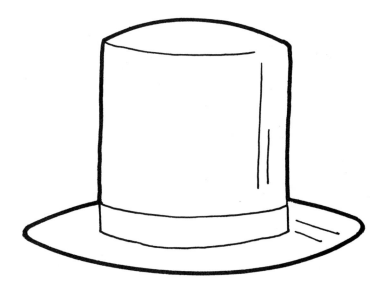

Black hat

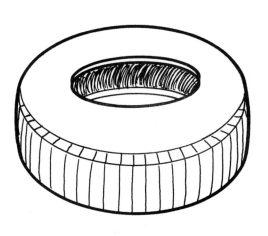

Black tire

Black bat

Black cat

Black, black, all around.

See the black things I have found.

White

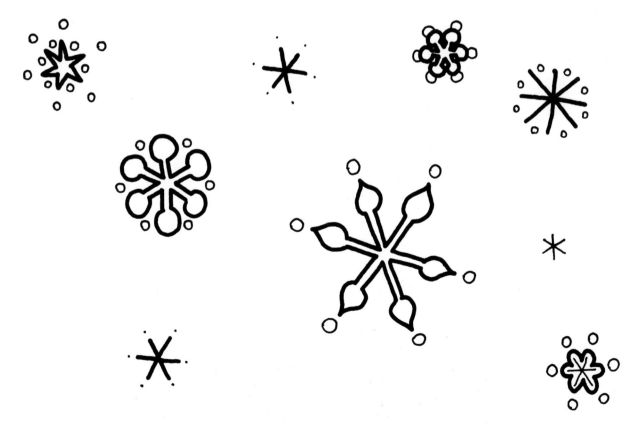

White snow

White cloud

MILK

White milk

White rabbit

White goose

White, white, all around.

See the white things I have found.

Shape Books

Circles

Clocks are circles.

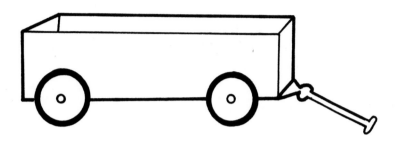

Wheels are circles.

Buttons are circles.

Cookies are circles.

Balls are circles.

Circles, circles, everywhere.

"I love circles," says the bear.

Squares

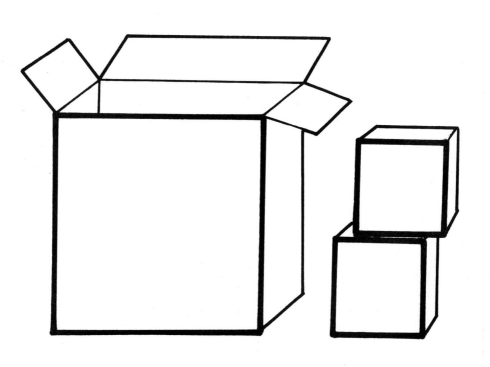

Boxes are squares.

Crackers are squares.

Signs are squares.

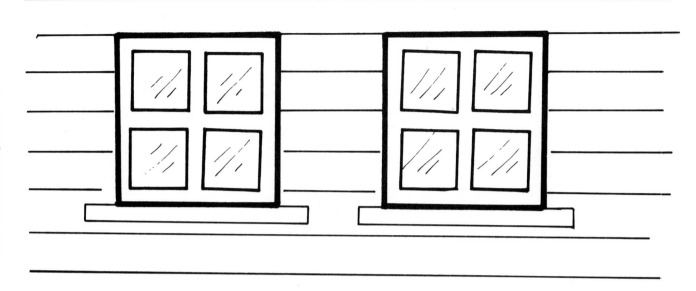

Windows are squares.

Blocks are squares.

Squares, squares, everywhere.

"I love squares," says the bear.

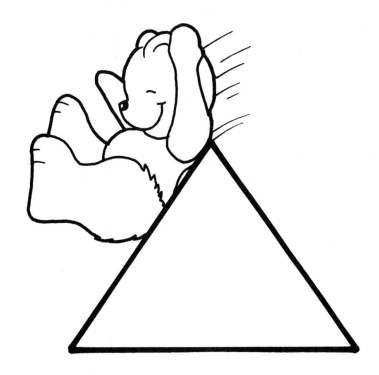

Triangles

Hats are triangles.

Tents are triangles.

Trees are triangles.

Sails are triangles.

Sandwiches are triangles.

Triangles, triangles, everywhere.

"I love triangles," says the bear.

Rectangles

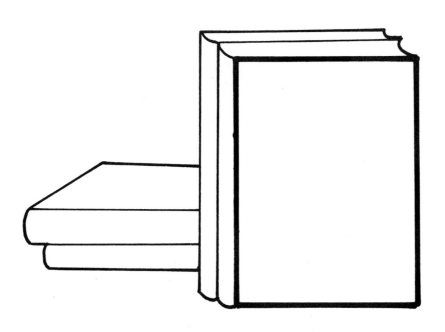

Books are rectangles.

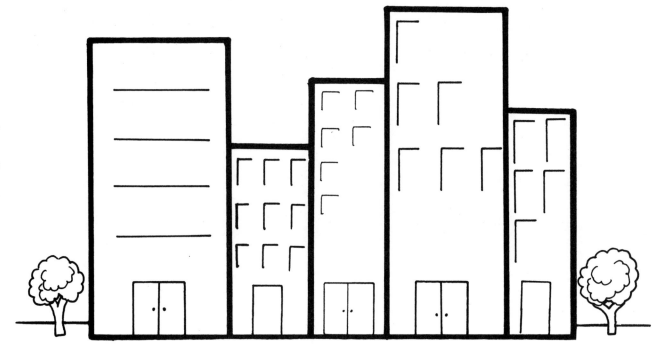

Buildings are rectangles.

Pictures are rectangles.

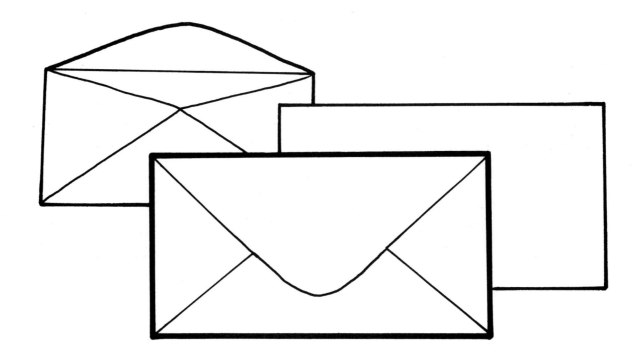

Envelopes are rectangles.

Doors are rectangles.

Rectangles, rectangles, everywhere.

"I love rectangles," says the bear.

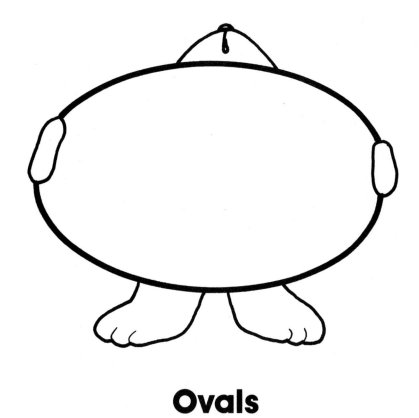

Ovals

Eggs are ovals.

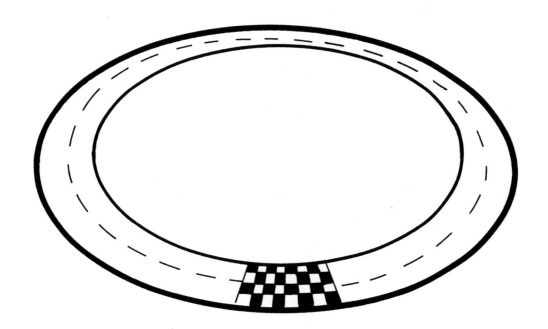

Race tracks are ovals.

Potatoes are ovals.

Bathtubs are ovals.

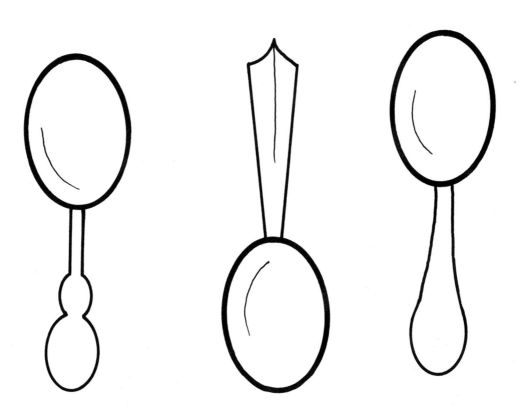

Spoons are ovals.

Ovals, ovals, everywhere.

"I love ovals," says the bear.

Season Books

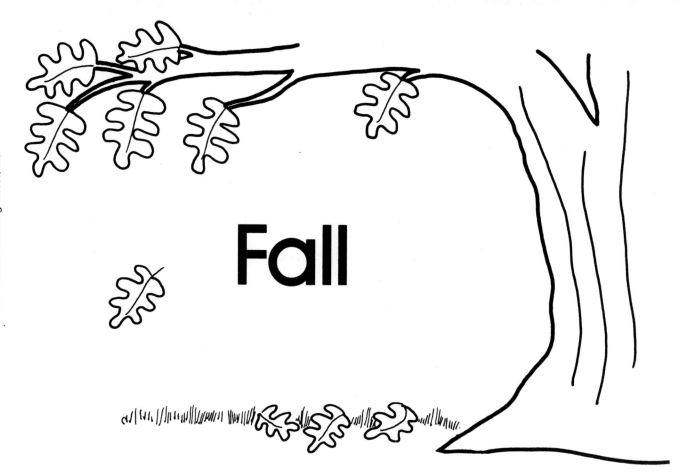

Fall

Fall leaves

Fall pumpkins

Fall spiders

Fall apples

Fall nuts

Fall, fall, under the tree.

How many fall things can I see?

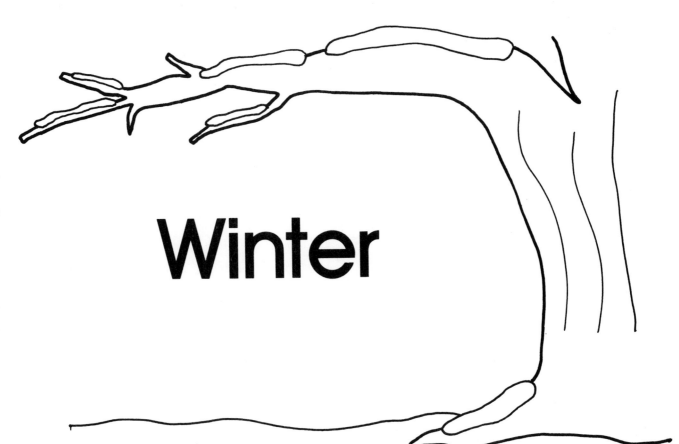

Winter

Winter snowflakes

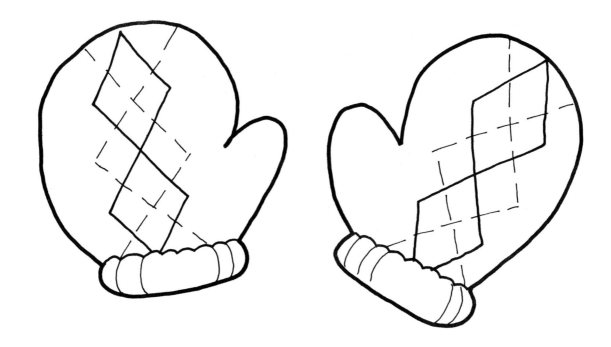

Winter mittens

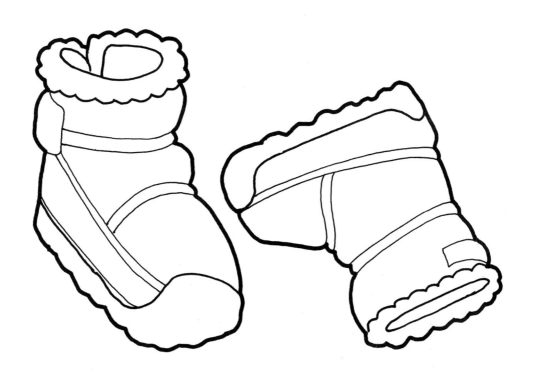

Winter boots

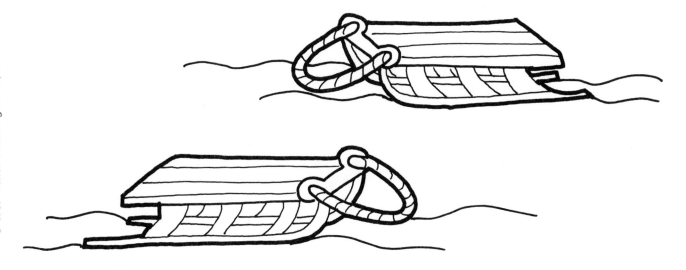

Winter sleds

Winter hats

Winter, winter, under the tree.

How many winter things can I see?

Spring

Spring flowers

Spring birds

Spring kites

Spring rain

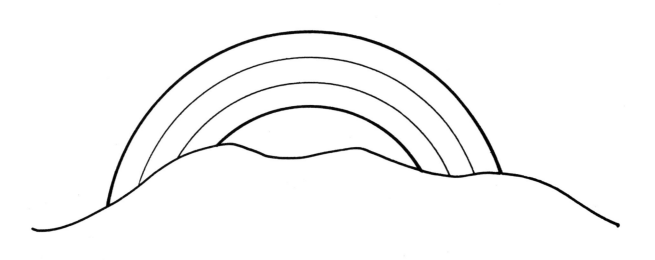

Spring rainbow

Spring, spring, under the tree.

How many spring things can I see?

Summer

Summer sun

Summer boats

Summer toys

Summer butterflies

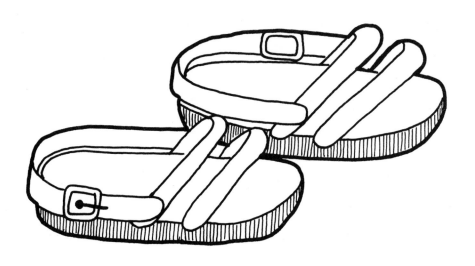

Summer shoes

Summer, summer, under the tree.

How many summer things can I see?

Totline® Newsletter

Activities, songs and new ideas to use right now are waiting for you in every issue!

Each issue puts the fun into teaching with 32 pages of challenging and creative activities for young children. Included are open-ended art activities, learning games, music, language and science activities plus 8 reproducible pattern pages.

Published bi-monthly.

Sample issue - $2.00

Super Snack News

Nutritious snack ideas, related songs, rhymes and activities

Published monthly.

Sample issue - $2.00

- Teach young children health and nutrition through fun and creative activities.

- Use as a handout to involve parents in their children's education.

- Promote quality child care in the community with these handouts.

- Includes nutritious sugarless snacks, health tidbits, and developmentally appropriate activities.

- Includes CACFP information for most snacks.

With each subscription you are given the right to:

Make up to: **200 COPIES** per issue

NEW! Exploring Books

Confused by the large number of new children's books published each year?

Need help in selecting just the right titles for your library or classroom needs?

Then you need *Exploring Books*, the children's book review for librarians and teachers of young children - each filled with over 50 reviews of new and theme related titles plus tips on using children's books to teach.

Published quarterly.

Sample issue - $2.00

Warren Publishing House, Inc. • P.O. Box 2250, Dept. Z • Everett, WA 98203

Totline® Books

Piggyback® Songs

More Piggyback® Songs

Piggyback® Songs
    for Infants and Toddlers

Piggyback® Songs
    in Praise of God

Piggyback® Songs
    in Praise of Jesus

Holiday Piggyback® Songs

Animal Piggyback® Songs

Piggyback® Songs for School

Piggyback® Sign to Sign

1·2·3 Art

1·2·3 Games

1·2·3 Colors

1·2·3 Puppets

1·2·3 Murals

1·2·3 Books

1·2·3 Reading & Writing

1·2·3 Rhymes, Stories & Songs

1·2·3 Math

Teeny-Tiny Folktales

Short-Short Stories

Mini-Mini Musicals

Small World Celebrations

Special Day Celebrations

Yankee Doodle
    Birthday Celebrations

Great Big Holiday Celebrations

"Cut & Tell"
    Scissor Stories for Fall

"Cut & Tell"
    Scissor Stories for Winter

"Cut & Tell"
    Scissor Stories for Spring

Alphabet Theme-A-Saurus®

Theme-A-Saurus®

Theme-A-Saurus® II

Toddler Theme-A-Saurus®

Alphabet & Number Rhymes

Color, Shape & Season Rhymes

Object Rhymes

Animal Rhymes

Our World

Our Selves

Our Town

Animal Patterns

Everyday Patterns

Holiday Patterns

Nature Patterns

ABC Space

ABC Farm

ABC Zoo

ABC Circus

1001 Teaching Props

Super Snacks

Available at school supply stores and parent/teacher stores or write for our catalog.

Warren Publishing House, Inc. • P.O. Box 2250, Dept. B • Everett, WA 98203